Clint Faraday
book forty
Dead Tired

Clint is talking with a man in the Lemon Grass Restaurante. The man says he doesn't know what's wrong with him, lately. He always seems to be dead tired. The doctors can't find anything wrong and have been prescribing vitamins and mild stimulants. He keeps having wild dreams that leave him exhausted. He's tired, but can't sleep in the daytime.

Two days later, he's dead. He died in his sleep – while driving his ATV.

Contents

About the author

CD Moulton has traveled extensively over much of the world both in the music business, where he was a rock guitarist, songwriter and arranger and in an import/export business. He has been everything from a bar owner to auto salvage (junkyard) manager, longshoreman to high steel worker, orchid grower to landscaper, tropical fish farmer to commercial fisherman. He started writing books in 1983 and has published more than 350 books as of January 1, 2023. His most popular books to date are about research with orchids, though much of his science fiction and fantasy work has proven popular. He wrote the CD Grimes, PI series, and the Det. Nick Storie series, Clint Faraday series, and many other works.

He now resides in Gualaca, Chiriqui, Panamá, where he writes books, plays music with friends, does research with orchids and medicinal plants. He has lately become involved in fighting for the rights of the indigenous people, who are among his closest friends, and in fighting the extreme corruption in the courts and police in Panamá.

He offers the free e-book, *Fading Paradise*, that explains what he has been through because of the corruption.

CD is the discoverer of the Chadam Protocol for curing cancer.

Facebook page Ambrosia peruviana for cancer.

Dead Tired

<u>*A Conversation*</u>

"You look tired, Ed," Clint Faraday, retired PI from Florida now residing in Panamá with his wife and two young children, said to Ed Williams, fellow resident. They were having a delicious dinner at The Lemon Grass, an excellent Thai restaurante in Bocas Town, Isla Colón, Bocas del Toro, Panamá. Clint lived on the island part of the year and on the Comarca Ngobe Bugle the rest of his time. He was only the second white person in history to be declared a Ngobe Indio, a fact of which he was very proud. His wife, Tyna (pronounced Teena) was a Ngobe. He was raising his chlidren, Nito (Clintonito), 3, and Nicole, 16 months, in the Indio tradition.

"I am. I'm exhausted all the time. They can't find why. I get a good night's sleep, eight to ten hours! I have these wild dreams and wake up exhausted. I've tried to take naps, but I could never sleep in the daytime.

"Doc Travis is the third one. He's giving me lots of stress vitamins and caffeine that helps some.

"I'm a little nervous about this. I wake up with bruises and cuts sometimes. In the dreams I'm running from something indefinite. I get in fights and guess I thresh around in my sleep because I wake up with the bruises and cuts.

"I'm beginning to think I need a psychiatrist, not a MD!"

"Carl Winters told me about your little run-in with Oscar Laske the other night. I suppose you got a bruise or two from that! He said you two smacked each other pretty good a couple of times."

"I know Carl, but who is Oscar Whatever? I haven't had any run-in with anybody! Which night was that supposed to be?

"Clint, I've had a couple of things people said about me that simply never happened! I don't know what's going on!"

"It was ... Wednesday night. About midnight. Out near the bluffs in that little local bar. Sami's. Carl said it was mostly you being macho."

"But ... Clint! I wasn't there! I was home! Asleep!"

"Did you wake up yesterday with bruises?"

"... Yes! Clint! I don't know what's going on! My ATV was used. It barely had enough gas to get to the bombas. I had more than three gallons Wednesday afternoon!

"I don't know what's happening to me! I'm scared!"

"We'll meet tomorrow at ten at The Grill. Tie yourself to the bed or something. Something that'll wake you up if you get out of bed. I think maybe you're a sleepwalker. Have you ever had any experiences like this before?"

"When I was fifteen and sixteen I would sometimes sleepwalk. I was sharing a room with my brother. He would wake me up. Once I was out by the road in my skivvies talking to a local pervert in his car. Andy woke me up and started giving me hell, but he woke me up several times in the house so he had an idea about what was happening. My folks had Dr. Ames check me out and he gave me some pills I was to take whenever I got the ... Clint! I get the jitters about four or five o'clock, just like I did then! He gave me some pills he said would suppress my, what he called my second personality. He said I had a cousin who had the same problem. My father said his mother would sleepwalk.

"If I can find out what pills I took maybe this would stop. I know I didn't like how they made me feel the next day and stopped taking them when I didn't get the afternoon jitters anymore. I only sleepwalked one other time that I remember. It was when I was writing my master's thesis. My roommate woke me up when I was having some kind of argument with another student in the hall. I didn't remember going out there and when he woke me ... I was confused and thought it was sleepwalking. I went to the clinic and told the doctor there about it and he gave me ... lithium! It was lithium!

"I took it four days and didn't get the jitters anymore and stopped taking it. Maybe I can get some lithium here and this shit will stop.

"Why didn't I remember that before now? Why didn't I think of it when it first started?

"Now I have to worry that I'm hiding something from myself! It should have been obvious! I've been getting the afternoon jitters and waking up tired for more than three weeks! My god!

"Clint, I don't know what's happening to me!"

"Get some lithium and put a stop to it. I think it won't be so bad. I've heard it makes you loggy the next day or something, but that's a lot better than exhaustion."

"You've got that right! I have to wonder why the bruises and cuts and if I've been getting into fights.

"Clint, what if this is schizophrenia? What if my other personality is ... Clint, my brother found me in a car with a known ... I have to say 'pervert,' because I was fourteen and he was in his thirties.

I also once, while I was in college, woke up in bed with a gay student. I didn't remember going there, but I was drinking and had a toke or two so didn't worry much about it.

"Carl isn't gay. I was supposed to be having a fight with him about some macho thing?

"Clint, what if my other personality is gay? I do notice when a man is particularly handsome. I've always noticed how the men here wear pants that look to me like they're ... empty. Like, I was always used to tighter pants that showed.... Why would I notice that? What have I been doing that ends me up with cuts and bruises?

"Now I'm really getting scared! It's not because my other personality might be gay. I really think I wouldn't mind so terribly much except there's a lot of AIDS here. I did have gay friends when I was in my teens and early twenties who I slept with, but always a one-way thing. I was always the pitcher, never the catcher – that I know about! Now I have that to wonder about!

"Why would ... who was I with that I don't remember? Am I going to meet people on the street who I've known that intimately and not remember? Will they think I'm snubbing them?

"Clint, this is weird! I was married fourteen years to Millie! We have three grown kids. Why didn't anything like that happen that whole time?

Why didn't my second personality, if I really have one, do anything for that time?"

"Maybe your second personality is bisexual and was content with the marriage. Have you always had a companion since Millie died?"

"Yes. Generally. I was never without a female companion for more than a couple of weeks. There were always the brothels for those times. I haven't had a live-in here for about three months. Glena and Flo cured me of Bocas women. I was waiting to meet someone who wasn't playing stupid games. I'm old enough at fifty three that I don't have that constant pressure like when I was twenty. I can do without for quite a long while now. Then, I'd be horny all the time. I only had two one-nighters in the past three months."

"So your alter ego is bi and doesn't care what kind of sex, just so there's sex. He's a sex addict. I've met a few."

"So. I'll get some lithium and come to terms with me. I like sex, but there's a limit."

"We'll meet in the morning. You can go to the hospital. Dr. Sandros will probably give you some lithium."

"I'll do that!"

<u>*It Was A Dream – Wasn't It?*</u>

Clint was waiting at The Grill when Ed showed up at five minutes after ten. In Panamá, that was like being two hours early. What Clint called "Panamanian time" was that way. Ten o'clock meant twelve or one – or tomorrow.

Ed looked more tired than last night. Clint asked why.

"I don't know! I went home and got nine hours of sleep and I'm more tired than ever! I did dream about a wild sexual party. We talked about that last night."

"The lithium didn't help?"

"Lith ... my god! I didn't even think of it until right now! I was so tired I drove right past the hospital on my way home. I almost went to sleep a couple of times on the way."

"So. What did you dream about? Maybe your alter ego is trying to get you into it so you won't suppress him. He has to know about the lithium.

"Ed, the way I understand it he knows everything you do. He knows we're talking right now. You don't know anything about him.

"If you're too strong to fight about things like

the lithium, he'll try to get you to want the same things he does. You've already said you're partway there.

"Tell me about the dream. Can you remember much of it?"

"I can remember a lot. More than before."

"What does your alter ego call himself? Do you know that? I may be able to reach him if what I've heard and seen holds."

"I don't ... Randy. It's not for Randolf, it's just Randy.

"How did I know that?"

"He has a sense of humor. He's Randy."

"Oh."

"Talk to me, Randy?"

Ed looked confused for a moment and shook his head.

"Okay. Tell me about the dream now, in as much detail as you can."

"I went home and changed into other ... so that's why that stuff was on the chair. I changed into more flashy and sexy clothes. I remember I was thinking shorts and a collar shirt would get a whore to offer something for pay and I wanted something that would attract someone else, for obvious reasons.

"I used the Ho Fai, not the ATV. I went out past the bluffs to a little bar the Indios use. There were about twenty people there. I knew a lot of them ... I'll be damned!"

"Go on. Don't comment now."

"Well, we had some beers. I was talking with a transvestite, Wanda, who I'd screwed a couple of times ... so that part's true!

"There were four other guys and two women. Girls in their early twenties, if that. One of them sat in my lap and started rubbing my leg. Ensa. I've screwed her before. And sixty nine.

"The tranny, the two girls and four guys and I went to Samuel's place. It was close and is big enough and his piece had left him for some guy on Popa.

"We had an all-night orgy is what it amounted to. The tranny, the two girls ... and Guillermo. He's a truly beautiful man. He ... we did a lot of things. He was pitching and I was catching. I remember thinking he would be one who could make me decide to ... to stay with one person.

"It broke up when we were all too tired to go on. I wanted to go home with Guillermo, but couldn't. I had to wake up at home. He wouldn't go for it anyway.

"I got home just as the sun was coming up and went to bed.

"That was a dream – wasn't it? Was it my alter ego letting me know what he's been doing?

"Clint, he's afraid he was actually falling in love with a man. With Guillermo!"

"Is Guillermo that Indio fellow who acts as a tourist guide at the airport?"

"I don't ... yes! My god! I always talk with him when we meet. Now I've ... maybe it was a dream. I always thought he was a very handsome man and he's got a great personality. It's certainly no secret that he's a gigolo for hire, but he seems selective. He gives the gringas who want to get laid by an Indio the big thrill. I know I've seen some of them who almost crawled around him when they're leaving.

"If I really did all the things I remember from the dream, I understand why! He can deliver the fantasy in surround sound, three-D and living color!

"It was a dream – wasn't it?

"I think I sort of hope it wasn't."

"I've heard others say he's more than a dream. He's a nice guy. He's clean and open and friendly and honest.

"I have a start to investigate what you've been doing. Maybe it'll be something that your alter ego and you can both enjoy. You'll have to work something out about the sleep, though. That's something.

"Get the lithium.

"Randy, just for tonight. We can work this out to

everyone's satisfaction, I think."

There wasn't any response. Ed left and Clint went home to his wife and children. They would spend the day on the water with their next door neighbor in Bocas Town, Judi Lum, and her boyfriend.

Judi was an oriental woman, exotic and very attractive. She and Clint had been friends since he moved to Bocas. She was a genius when it came to getting information. She had helped on a lot of his cases.

They had a good time going among the islands and stopping to chat with friends. They stopped on a little island about noon to have a good picnic, then went on toward Chiriqui Grande and started back. They all talked about their projects and what had been happening. Clint told them a little about Ed's problem.

"Janiz says he was out toward Drago one night, about a week ago. He was with a local girl, Dona Something, and three men. Two Indios and one Panamanian. They spent the night in a little house next to where she and Moises live. She said by the sounds of it they had a wild night. She said she thinks everybody did everything to everybody else!

"I thought she must be mistaken. Ed is a sorta sedate kind of person."

"When he's Ed. Sometimes he's Randy."

"He sure was Randy enough that night if it was him!"

"I guess. Maybe we can work something out where his health won't go down the drain. The body can only stand so much."

They talked about other things and enjoyed the day. They were caught up on local happenings and delivered messages to people from their friends and relatives on the comarca. They got back just before dark. Judi and Bino went into town for dinner. Clint spent the time relaxing with his family. He used to be in town looking almost every night, then he married Tyna and was content. He had literally millions of dollars in the bank and was spending it helping his people, the Indigenos. He could lay around or run around all he wanted and never worry where the money for any of it would be.

He probably would spend a lot less time in Bocas Town and a lot more on the comarca.. Here, he would get up to watch the sunrise with his coffee and his son and daughter on his lap. They would spend the day on the water or on the islands trying to find something to do.

On the comarca he would get up to watch the sunrise with his son and daughter on his lap, then would go to help cut wood or work the gardens or build a house for someone or ten thousand other things.

It was a sort of basic philosophy. He felt he was wasting his time outside the comarca except when he had a mystery to solve. For a short time he would have a purpose, a place, in Bocas. He always had a place on the comarca.

He looked at it as having two things he could spend. Time and money. The difference was that he could always get more money so it made no difference if he wasted a lot of it. He had a fixed amount of time that couldn't be changed. A fool, and only a fool, would waste much of it.

When he first came to Panamá it had become an immediate paradise for him. He had enough to buy this house and to fish and lay around with a little mystery to solve now and then. He went around the country to see new places and meet new people. He met and helped a couple of the Indios on Isla San Cristóbal and had become enamored of their culture. It was inclusive, while all he had ever known before was exclusive.

A very powerful gangster had come there on a case and had known this was the place he could raise a family who wouldn't be ashamed of how Pops made his. He was now another who worked with the local people and respected and was respected by them. He had found his place. Clint had found his place.

Had Judi found her place?

Really, Clint thought, she had. She worked with him in the detective bit and with the projects to help the Indigenos. She had more friends than ever before. She was loved and respected by the people. She liked plants and their mutual friend, the nutty author/botanist/musician, had her place (and Clint's – and Ben and Earl's) covered with exotic orchids and anthuriums and bromelliads and whatever. She was attractive with a great personality. She was living life exactly the way she wanted it.

Yes. Judi had found her place.

Clint hugged and teased his kids. Tyna came out from cleaning up the kitchen to start teasing at Clint. Nito said it was time for all that sex stuff he didn't know or care about so he would take Nicole to their bedroom and go to bed.

That was another thing about the Indio culture. No one tried to hide the facts of life from the young kids. They were around cows and pigs and chickens and all other kinds of natural things. They saw what nature was. They knew they were going to reach an age where they were interested in such things. They didn't fear or dread it. It was going to happen. It wasn't "wrong" or "evil" and they weren't going to hell because they were human. Clint remembered when Marta, a super-religious woman, had declared, "They're bound straight for hell!" about a young man and woman who decided to move in together. Nito was a little less than four years old. He asked why.

"They are breaking God's law! They will pay the penalty!"

"But why would God make people to want that and then put them in hell because they did what he made them to do?"

"Satan draws them away! It is Satan who makes them do that!"

"But you said only God could make things. If Satan draws them to what God made them, why would they go to hell? It doesn't make any sense to me."

"You little heathen!"

Clint couldn't stop himself. He laughed out loud. She swore at him and marched haughtily away. Clint explained to Nito that there were all kinds. She was certainly one of them.

"If that's the kind everybody is in heaven I don't want to go there."

Clint thought a second. "You have a point."

They went home where it was warm inside.

In the morning just after sunrise Sergio, head of the Bocas police, called.

"Clint? Sergio here. You were talking with Ed Williams yesterday and day before about some kind of problem or other?"

"Yes. He sleepwalks. It leaves him tired all the time. I think he's schizophrenic."

"He's dead."

"What?!"

"He was coming from somewhere out past The Bluffs on his ATV and went over where that bad washout is by the river. It was about four o'clock. He was apparently going too fast."

"Randy trying to get home before dawn."

"What?"

"Nothing. Thanks, Sergio."

"That's not all. Enrique Valdero was sleeping it off not fifty feet away across the road under that ledge. He woke up when he heard something and saw him go over. He said Ed had stopped and was talking to someone and that he suddenly just went over. He thinks the person he was talking to pushed him over."

"He was sober enough for it to be what he actually saw? He wasn't hallucinating?"

"No. He's sober. He'd slept there since before midnight. He wasn't too drunk when he went to sleep. It was starting to rain so he went under the ledge.

"There's something else. Doc said he had a very hard blow to the back of the head before he went over."

"Any description of the man?"

"Sort of big and maybe dark. Wearing a yellow raincoat."

"So. Someone was waiting there for Ed. The raincoat to make him think it was police. He stopped."

"And there was something in the road, Riko thinks. A big box or something. He says it was to the side where he didn't get a good look at it. He stayed quiet and waited for the man to leave and came to the phone at the intersection by the casita to call us."

"I'll come in. Half an hour."

He rang off and sat to think. Nito asked if he was going to work.

"Yeah, I think so." He put on some clothes and told Tyna he had a case. Ed Williams was dead.

"From?"

"Murder's my guess. That's why I'm going in."

"Okay. Be careful."

He went into town and to the station, where Sergio was waiting for the ME's medical report. Riko was there to talk with them about what happened.

"I was sleeping, but it was time to wake up anyhow. I could hear, but there were clouds. I couldn't see very much. Only shadows.

"I didn't pay much attention, but there was a man in a yellow poncho waiting across the road. There was something big and square on the road maybe fifteen meters on toward Drago.

"The red moto came and went very slow and the man went out right where the piece of the road has washed away and stopped the moto. He said some things, maybe a little loud, but that was possibly because the moto makes some noise.

"Then there were two sort of a 'gngh!' sounds at almost the same time and another sound like when someone hits someone with his fist, then the moto went over the side.

"I knew the big man did something bad and I'm just a little old man so I was very quiet. The man went toward Drago and took the square thing with him. I waited and went to the telephone at the casita and called Sergio."

"You said the man was dark?" Clint asked.

"I only think so. I did not see white, but it may

have been a dark shirt and his back was always to where I was."

"You couldn't hear what they said?"

"I could hear some. It was only eighteen or twenty meters away."

"Can you repeat any of it?"

"No. It was not in Spanish and I think not in English. Maybe ... I don't know. Not French or Italian. More like Russian, but not that, I think."

He didn't know much more. He soon went home and Clint and Sergio went to Don Chicho's for coffee and hojaldres. They were back in the station forty minutes later when Doc called and said maybe they'd better come to the morgue.

They took the police truck.

"He was stabbed. Not fatally, but in the side, where it cut a little into the lower liver. The mark on the back of the neck was from what I'd call a judo chop.

"There were two blood types on the ATV. One is Williams'. One isn't."

Sergio looked thoughtful. "Two 'gngh!' sounds almost together," Clint said.

"Yes. I think we will be looking for someone with a stab wound," Sergio replied. "It wasn't Spanish or English. Probably not a romance language. I think we will necessarily need to seek a lot of information about Edward Williams."

He took out his radio and ordered his fellow officers to thoroughly canvass all the bars and so forth from The Bluffs to Boca del Drago. See where Edward Williams had been and who he was seen with.

"Randy," Clint said.

"What?"

"He would be using the name, Randy."

Sergio added that. They collected copies of Doc's photos and reports and went back to the station to consider what they knew to the point.

"It was supposed to look like a reckless driver and we wouldn't look further. Riko made us take the very close look," Sergio suggested. "Perhaps our culprit isn't aware we know he has suffered a stab wound?"

"Yes. Keep it quiet."

Sergio called Doc and said not to tell anyone they knew anything. Certainly no report of a stab wound, possibly only that there was a mark on his neck that could or could not mean anything.

Clint got on the computer and started his trace of Williams. Two hours later he declared that Williams might be into any number of things, but he wasn't an agent for any government and he wasn't on any witness protection program.

"He grew up in a normal neighborhood in a

small town, went to college for four years, got an engineering degree, worked as a civil engineer in the US, Australia, Brazil, and Yemen.

"That will be it, but what is it?

"Sergio, are there any Yemeni here?"

"None that I'm aware of." He went to the main intersystem computer to ask immigration if there were any Yemeni in the country. It seemed there were several, but all in Panamá City so far as they knew.

"There's at least one who isn't anywhere near Panamá City," Clint remarked. Sergio nodded.

"We're looking for a Yemeni sporting a stab wound. There would have to be very few here," Sergio said. "He will have to use a boat or plane to leave."

He called the airport immigration and checked. No Yemeni had come in or gone out within the past three months. By plane.

"Boat. Already headed for the canal," Sergio said sourly. Clint thought and said maybe not. Maybe he had some place he could stay on Isla Colón until a wound healed.

"If he's here, we'll find him. Particularly if he doesn't know we're looking for him.

"I think perhaps Judi will be our best way to determine if he's here."

Clint couldn't argue with that!

After checking everything they had on anyone from that area of the world Clint went home. Sergio had called Judi. She'd probably call back in ten minutes with information it would take them a week to find.

Tyna had made a curry pizza that their close friend, Dave, had sort of invented for dinner, with a salad. He relaxed on the deck with the kids for a little while, then they walked into Bocas Town. When they were passing Mondo Taitu four Rastas came out to pull their intimidation act. That went over with Clint like, as he said, a pregnant pole-vaulter.

Most of the Rastas were regular people in Bocas. A few like these were total assholes. They had a white man and an Indio woman and two small children.

"Gimme five dollars, white trash, or I fuck you woman right in fronta you babies!" one of them demanded.

"Kiss my royal rusty ass, pigshit!" Clint responded.

"You've got that one tagged!" Travis, a black man who was a good friend for the whole time Clint had been there, said. He said something to the Rastas in Wadi-Wadi. One of them drew a knife. The one with the mouth.

"Here we go again!" Nito said. "Don't kill these

cruds, Dad. I don't want to have to sit in the police station half the night like last time."

Nito was just a little more than four years old, but was fast in his thinking and often sounded like he was a lot older. Travis winked at them. Tyna said, "Yes. Clint, if you want to kill them let us go on so we don't have to go through all that again. It's such a bore!"

"They're not kidding!" Travis warned.

The one with the knife lunged at Clint, who had the training. He grabbed his arm and twisted up, then brought it down hard against his knee. The knife went skittering across the pavement while the three other Rastas looked scared and Travis giggled evilly. The would-be knife artist squealed in a very high pitch. Clint thought he might have broken an arm there. Tyna rolled her eyes and said, "Come on Nito. We haven't seen anything here.

"We'll see you back at the house in the morning I guess, Love. Don't get all bloody like last time. It takes hours to get the blood out of your clothes! Show a little consideration!"

Four backpackers came out of the Taitu and were staring at the scene. The other three Rastas went running down the road. The one with the knife was whining. Nito picked up the knife and said he was going to add it to his collection. He waved and Tyna took him and Nicole and went on toward the park

Travis was laughing like crazy. The backpackers were staring. It was like some scene from those stupid violence flicks on TV.

Clint grabbed a handful of dredlocks and stared at the Rasta from six inches away.

"If you ever say anything like that to another person and I hear about it make the arrangements because I'm going to kill you slower and more painfully than you would ever believe possible. If I ever hear you or any other of your type of shit say stronger than 'darn it!' in front of my wife or children it goes for them.

"Got it?"

"I was just...."

Clint bounced his head against the pavement. "Got it?"

"Yeah! Yeah! I got it!"

"Well! Hi, Trav. How's things?"

"Regular, Clint. You?"

"Nothing new. The same old same old." They walked away toward town. The backpackers were standing there with their mouths hanging open. The Rasta was moaning. When they were out of hearing of the backpackers, Clint said, "Trav, we have to do something to stop that kind of crap. It's ruining this place!"

"Little Nito came off with that ... I'm always amazed at your kids. Most kids are saying 'Mah-ma!' and 'Dah-da' at the age he was saying 'Hey, Mom! Trav is here!' He's a genius!"

"He's just an Indio kid. You have some Indio relatives. You even speak the dialect better than a lot of them."

"I was raised black. I was just like them when I was that age. I've spent fifteen years trying to get that culture out of me."

They chatted as they walked on to the parque, where Tyna was talking with Judi. Nito ran to Clint and hugged him. "I was scared! You always said those Colón people are all bluff. Did I do right?"

"You did perfect!" Travis replied. "You made it seem like Clint had to kill those kinds of shits at least once a week. I'll get the word out that they'd better go back to Colón and they'd better stay there. Clint doesn't give second warnings."

"I don't!" Clint shot back. Travis gave him the finger and laughed. He waved and went toward the Toro Loco. Clint went to Tyna and Judi.

"Clint, I'm so proud of Nito I don't know what to do! I was about to scream or something and he came up with that, so I played along.

"I told Esteban. He's going to pick them all up. I told him the one was probably in the hospital.

He knows who the other three are. He'll hold them three days for investigation and they have to leave the island. If they don't leave within four hours another officer will pick them up for three more days of investigation. They can keep that going until they get the point.

"Judi says Sergio asked her to find some things. She can tell you about it."

"Hi, Jude! What's the skuttle?" Clint greeted.

"Other than some macho gringo viejo kicking fifty Rastas' asses at the Mondo Taitu, nothing. What's with you?"

Clint laughed. "There you go! Exaggerating again! It was only forty seven of them!"

"Clint, we have to do something about the violence here. It keeps getting worse!"

"They have to stop treating them like wayward children and start treating them like what they are. Criminals. Let's not get into that now. Have you learned anything about our Yemeni?"

"Not really, but there's been a man seen around that Iranian store. He says he's Turkish, but he's not. Akmed is Turkish and says he doesn't speak five works of their language. He looks and acts more Greek.

"They call him Mek. He doesn't come out very often. He's been here about two weeks and no one knows where he's staying, which means he's got friends or contacts here he's staying with. He hasn't been seen out of town, but that doesn't mean he hasn't been out of town."

"Too true. Maybe Sergio can find something."

"I know who you mean," Nito said. "He's Nekah's uncle. He's from Palestine. He stays on their boat. He acts mean, but he's not. Seleth says he acts that way because that's how he was raised. He was at the beach one day."

"Hey!" Judi cried, laughing. "What? You're after my job?

"Clint, you're lying about his age. He's twenty two, not two!"

"Get on your balls!" Nito fired back.

"I ain't got balls. That's get on *the* ball," Judi replied.

"Get on whatever it is. I don't have time to do your job and mine too! I'm only a kid. Sheesh!"

"I think Tyna spends all her time teaching him what to say," Clint said. "He's using a lot of my expressions."

"In a way, that's right," Tyna said. "He keeps asking me what this or that means. He heard you or somebody else saying it.

"Nito, did the uncle say why he's here?"

"No. He didn't talk much. Nekah says he's just here because of something somebody said on the net. He's always on the net and that made him get in trouble."

That was about all they could learn. Clint warned Nito not to let anyone know he told them anything or that he even knew anything. They changed the subject and talked about other things. After awhile Clint and family went home.

"Sergio, did you bring that computer from Ed's house here?" Clint asked the next morning.

"Yes. I always collect that kind of thing in these circumstances. I brought it, several memory sticks and a lot of CD's. Important?"

"Could be. Nekah's uncle, a Palestinian who's staying on Nekah's father's boat that's moored over near the marina, is here because of something he found on the net that got him in trouble. Seleth says he only acts mean because he was raised that way, but he really isn't."

Sergio stared at him a moment. "It will never fail to amaze me how Judi gets this kind of thing in a few minutes – while talking about something else. That would take us a week, at least."

"Oh, Judi only found the part where Mek says he's from Turkey, but he doesn't speak a word of Turkish."

"You have someone better than Judi?! I don't believe you!"

"Some little kid by the name of Nito plays with Nekah and Mek was on the beach with them one day and he was okay and Nekah said all that other stuff when they were playing later."

"And no one is careful what they say around a little kid. Tell him to be very careful, Clint. The man's a killer. He probably wouldn't hesitate to get rid of anyone who knows too much, including little kids."

"I impressed that on him last night when we got home. He's sharp enough to know it was serious."

"He's a genius. I don't care what you say!"

"I'm almost convinced myself.

"Let's crank up that comp and see what we can find!"

They went into the evidence vault and got the computer and hardware and took it into Sergio's office. Six hours later they weren't sure whether they had anything or not. It was all hints dug out from several sources and put together.

"He has a blog somewhere in someone else's name," Sergio decided. Clint agreed.

"Okay, we have to trace back since he was in Yemen. That was seven years ago until five years eight months ago. He was there on an exploratory trip for an investment group. He was designing some kind of ... something.

"We have to find that group and what they're into. There's damned little information about that time. All we have is Yemen, not even a place in Yemen. He was designing something we don't have ... Sergio! Those instructional CDs! What were they about?"

"The language and some topographical studies and high pressure storage vessels, mostly."

"We can assume that he learned the language. He was heard talking in it. Topographical studies was probably satellite stuff they use looking for oil. High pressure storage. Natural gas? There's plenty of that in the area, but there's plenty in a lot of places. I don't get it!

"I want to look at those topographical things. I want to see where he was concentrating. There was a sounding study that didn't show me much. I don't even know if it's for that area."

After half an hour he knew Ed had concentrated on an area of low sand hills and smaller rocks. The satellite views showed a typical well drilling truck working there for a couple of months. Clint got as closeup a view as was possible with the equipment and counted the lengths of pipe being used.

"Sergio, that's just three inch pipe! It's more than a mile of it!

"What's with the stacks of two inch?

"Okay. It's sand there with a little rock on top. There was a sounding map. I want to study that. It showed a sort of gas dome at about that depth. I suppose three inch pipe would deliver a hell of a lot of gas at high pressure. My question is 'Why?'

when there's so much available that a lot of gas wells are capped now!"

"Clint, what's this?" Sergio asked and pointed to a moving camera shot on his screen. It was shown as a stop-and-start movie of approaching a few rocks. From a distance it was just that. As it got closer there was a sort of fog around the rocks. Closer it was a denser fog. Closer it was all fog. Then there were pictures of mutated plants and mutated insects.

Clint whistled. "Let's find out what we can about that investment company!"

"What is it?"

"I don't know, but it's scary as all hell to me! I think I know what that smaller pipe is about!"

"All that ... radioactive gas? They're found a gas dome that's contaminated with radioactives? They want to extract the radioactives?"

"I don't think so. I really don't think so.

"Let's find that company!"

They found some notes on a CD that didn't seem to have any connection with anything there. Clint went back through and wrote all of them down. It came out "hattop willies patience dorothy secret typesetter news attention phase connector periodic organic."

He typed in www dot.pa.secrettypesetternews at phasecon dot org into the search bar. A website came up that was all about a typesetters union who were fighting computer printing. It was just plain silly, but the net was full of those. Physical type-setting was gone for good. A computer could do a day's work typesetting in about five minutes.

"That's not it," Sergio said.

"No!! Really?!?" He got the finger.

Clint typed in several more things taken from the code. He finally ended up with secretpenews at phasecon.org showing on the screen. It was a blog-type site run by Kingedward2007uptown. It was about a search for radon gas in quantity.

"Radon? Doesn't it have a rather short half-life?" Sergio asked.

"Relatively, but it's still dangerous concentration for ten years. They only need it for a week or so."

"Sergio, I don't know what we've found, but I have a very sick feeling in my gut! I want to know what's around or under that dome! It has to be something that produces radon in atomic break-down.

"Why isn't it critical mass? I don't get it!"

"The compression at a mile or more deep would be something else!" Sergio declared. "What have they found? Why isn't that dome itself more than critical mass?"

"Radon gas would have to be compressed to a liquid to form critical mass. Probably not even then. Whatever's producing it has to already be 'way more than critical! It doesn't make sense!"

"Not if it's a very large mass of porous material with whatever's breaking down spread through it to where it's just under critical mass. Radium and uranium ores are that."

"Shit! This is getting worse than scary!"

"I don't see...?"

"Radon gas in huge quantity. A way to compress and store it. What kind of threat could you make on almost anywhere in the world if you had a few cylinders of it in all the major cities? Turn a valve and everyone within a few miles ends up with radiation poisoning and half of them die of lung and bone cancer within five years?"

"Jesus H. Christ!"

"If we ever had something that had to be stopped with the end justifying the means, this is it!"

"So the far east is the threat again, but as much to themselves as to anyone else. I hate this!"

"Yeah. Every time we think we've found the ultimate stupidity from the far east we get another tale that's even worse.

"Sergio, we have to find some way to stop this. It's all too probably already too late!"

"Too late?"

"He's been here more than five years."

"But the satellite photos show they've only been

drilling for a month or so. They have to go ... how deep?"

Clint brought up the sounding, then went to the latest photo of the drilling rig.

"Okay. They've used about a third of a mile of pipe in a month. They have to go slow there. It's probably sand compressed to sandstone, but it's silica sand that will eat up the drill head if you get in a hurry. They haven't started inserting the lead pipe yet. We should have three or four months before they can be in production. Maybe we can do it!"

"Lead pipe? What are you talking about?"

"The two inch will be lead. If they started piping up that much radioactive gas the leakage through iron pipe would show like a beacon to the satellite. That was probably Ed's main job. Getting it up without it showing to the satellites that are there for radiation detection.

"I think that what happened was that Ed was given a job he thought was for another purpose. When we find ... so the so-called investment group will be a front for someone. It'll probably be some supposed medical research thing."

"It should be easy enough to trace. It will be the sponsor of that website."

"Or it will be the sponsor of something to get rid of that website and anyone who knows what it's about?"

Sergio shook his head. "Why in hell do you keep getting Panamá involved in these stupid international intrigues? Why can't you, as Dave says in those Nick Storie mysteries, get a case where some drunk guy says, 'I got pissed and blew the bastard's head off for him and whatcha gonna do about it, flatfoot!' instead of this crap where the whole world's at risk or worse?"

"Dave! Yes! I have to get in touch with Dave!"

"What now?"

"He did a lot of research on this kind of thing for that *After the Old Gods* book. Maybe he'll know what companies are backing research into this kind of thing!"

"Now we get nutcase authors involved. Whoopie shit!" That got him the finger.

Clint looked at the clock. It was almost midnight. He called Tyna and explained that something had come up that was beyond terrifying. They might move to Quebrada Tula permanently if this couldn't be stopped.

He started to call Dave, who was god-only-knew where. It was midnight. He would be asleep somewhere in a jungle or would be working with his laptop recording what he'd found that day. Or something.

He said, "What the hell?" and called. The second set (it went to voicemail after five rings. Dave had never been able to figure how to retrieve those messages and didn't want to) was answered. There was a lot of noise in the background.

"Where are you?" Clint asked.

"At Ja Rock, in David. I played. I'm just packing it up to go home."

"I have to get some information and I have to get it fast."

"What? I don't keep up with what you're doing. It gets way too complicated.

"Are you in Tula or Cusapín or where?"

"Bocas. We have something that scares the holy living shit out of Sergio and me."

"Nothing scares Sergio. What?"

"Huge amounts of radon gas."

"What? Chernobyl or another one of those?"

"Those little nothings? No. I can't talk about it on the phone. You may have some information I can use to find who's behind it. They'll probably be hiding behind a medical research company of some sort. They'll have some reason to want a large source of radon."

There was a silence. Finally Clint said, "Dave?"

"I'm trying to think. I remember looking at a lot of websites back before dot com. I remember a couple of things where they were looking for a specific radioactive that would target specific organs or such. Like iodine against thyroid cancer.

"I don't remember radon ... but there were some government agencies doing research on that kind of thing. We all know perfectly well what kind of use it would be put to by a government. *Curing* cancer would be among the last.

"I know that German group were into cures. They did some good things, but they weren't government funded by any wild stretch of the imagination.

"England. Russia. Israel. China. They're all still into that kind of warfare. I think Israel would have the most to fear if anyone else got something like that first."

"Yeah. They're probably out of it for that reason."

"Zionists? You're kidding, right? They operate always on the theory that you should hit the other guy before he hits you. Call it a pre-emptive hit and it's peachy keen and alright. The end *always* justifies the means! You're the terrorists, we're freedom fighters. Yeah. Right!"

"Let's not get into antiSemitism. I need data."

"AntiSemitism? I'm antiZionist. My god, look how Reichman and Silverberg and Levin have helped us with our projects! They're even more antiZionist than I am. They're Jews!

"Well, they're not Semitic, either. Look at them!

"What do you need?"

"I have to be able to trace a company or an organization that's found a huge source of radon gas that they're planning to compress and store. You know what that would have to be for."

"I doubt they could find enough concentrated radon gas to compress into one cylinder, much less what would be needed for that kind of lunacy. What leaks from the plant accidents altogether wouldn't fill a cylinder. It's only needed in small amounts. It's deadly as hell, but there just simply isn't that much to be had.

"Okay. Someone's obviously found a source, meaning I'm wrong. I'm wrong only about eighty five or ninety percent of the time."

"Dave, it was a long time ago that you wrote *After the Old Gods*, so ... how can I find this one?"

"Go to Google or Yahoo! and search radioactive medical research. Everything on the web will come up, he said, facetiously, and you can maybe find the one you want. The lists will name the backers of the research somewhere on the site."

"Thanks, Dave. You don't know how serious this is."

"Compressed radon in quantity? I don't know? When you could take a hair spray can of it into any population center and contaminate every single person within fifty yards of you?"

"I wish that was all it is, but try a big oxygen-type cylinder in every major city. Go upwind and turn a valve."

"I think I'll join you in Cusapín or somewhere. I'll have to study prevailing winds to be able to say if it would be reasonably safe. I do understand, Clint. I hope you can prevent it. Flippancy is a defense mechanism that kicks in automatically when I'm scared."

They said a little more, then Clint rang off and brought up Google. Three hours later he had gone to more than a hundred sites. He was dead tired and about to give it up until morning – well, later in the morning. It was two twenty four AM – when he came on Group2007.resrmed.com/radon/view. He went to the site to find it was backed by The Medicalistic Research Group, Ltd.

That sounded British enough!

He went to their site to find it was closed for maintenance until noon, Haifa time.

It was an Israeli group?

Mek was Palestinian. Wasn't he? Was this some group operating out of Israel, but against Israel?

Then he wondered if maybe Mek didn't know that was the group sponsoring him.

Clint went home to sack out until he woke up. He would be on that website as soon as it re-opened.

Was it possible they knew he was looking at them? Was it possible the website was closed until they could purge any information that wouldn't be to their advantage?

Maybe he knew a trick or two about that!

Clint woke up at nine twenty and went into the kitchen. Tyna, Judi and three women from the garden club were there. He said, "Good morning!" and poured a cup of the waiting coffee.

"Clint? We have guests?" Tyna said.

"Yes?"

"Put on some clothes, stupid!" Judi ordered. He had forgotten he was nude. He never dressed in the mornings until he knew what he was going to do for the day.

Nito came in carrying Nicole. He rolled his eyes and said Dad shouldn't be trying to sex up other women when Mom was there!

He blushed and went into the bedroom to slip on some shorts. He went back out to apologize, then onto the deck with his laptop. He took care of his e-mail and such and studied what he could find about radon. A lot of it was over his head. He did find that it was a very dangerous thing in even very minute amounts. Not like plutonium, but worse than iodine. It was inhaled and was in direct contact with the lung tissue. It was a problem with phosphate mining, as it was always in the deposits in very small quantities, but caused enormous health problems a few years down the line to those exposed to it for too long or in any concentration.

He finished that and sat back. The women left. Tyna soon brought him a bowl of lobster chowder and sat with Nicole. Nito came in and climbed into the hammock to lay against his chest. They talked about the case. Nito said he thought Mek was going to go home. Nekah said he was packing things and his father had an argument about something he did on the boat.

Clint called Sergio and said to stop him from going anywhere. Sergio said that he didn't have grounds, but with this one he'd invent a reason.

It was twelve ... and that had been Haifa time! It was twelve there ten hours ago!

He went to the website to find a lot of technical data about using radon in certain cases where all else had failed. There had been some success, but they didn't have nearly enough of the gas to use in conducting experiments. Storage was the basic problem. Delivery to the part of the body being treated was a very touchy thing, as it was a gas. It would leak into the air, giving everybody close a dose of radiation. The company was, supposedly, trying to find a storage and delivery method. It was an inert and would pass through any filter oxygen would pass.

He wasn't really interested in that. He'd found the information already in ten different places.

The group was several doctors at prestigious hospitals in Israel, Switzerland and the USA. He looked them up.

One name seemed vaguely familiar. He did a Google search on his name and found that he was arrested in the US twice for agitating against two different national politicians, both of whom were questioning the US funding projects for the Israeli government. He was a radical Zionist.

There's such a thing as a non-radical Zionist? Clint thought. *Wasn't that Dave's point?*

He looked up the names of the others he could find. They were all Zionists, but not the extreme type.

Okay. What was Mek doing messed up in it? Clint dressed and told the family he was off to the station.

He got to the station just as Esteban and Nando brought in a bullish man who looked Arabian to Clint. He asked, "Mek?"

"Yes? Do I know you?"

"No. I'm Clint Faraday. My son is a friend of Nekah's and described you to me. You're Nekah's uncle or something."

He smiled. "Ah, yes! The children. They will think I'm an ogre, I suppose?"

"Nito said you try to act mean, but you're alright. You can't even act mean in a convincing way."

He laughed. "So I am found out! The children are wise and I'm the fool not to see that I do not fool them!"

"Children and dogs always seem to know," Clint agreed.

"Children, yes. I can fool dogs. I am seldom fooled by people."

"Some people are very professional at fooling others."

"I feel there is a reason to say this?"

"Yes. Let's go inside. I think maybe you're being used by the very last people you would be used by."

"Enigmatic!" He waved to the door and followed Clint in. Esteban said they wouldn't be needed anymore so would go back on patrol. Sergio came and they went to his office. Clint asked for coffee and offered Mek some.

"So. Who am I being fooled by?"

"Zionists," Clint answered. Mek suddenly got a very hard look about him.

"I do not think those pigs can fool me!"

"They are The Medicalistic Research Group, Ltd."

"No! The group is from Beirut! I have been in their offices many times! They are Palestinian and Lebanese!"

Clint turned the computer around and went online to the group's site. He pointed to the names of the officers, which were mostly neutral types of names that could be from almost anywhere. He pointed to "Dr. M. Green, MD-GP" and went to Google to bring up the name. The part about him being arrested twice for agitating against anti-Zionist people was right there. He brought up two

others and he brought up that the main headquarters of the group was in Haifa. He thought
Mek would die of apoplexy on the spot.

"So. I am twice the fool! I will have my revenge!
They will die in agony!

"What have I done? Why did...?"

"Why did they have you kill Ed? Because he was
about to tell the world who they were and what
they were doing?" Sergio replied. "Clint, that's
why the code on the CDs. I really think it was!"

"I agree. What can we do now?

"Mek ... what's your name?"

"Mek will do. What my passport says is farther
from the actuality."

"Okay. What they plan is what they will do. It
just won't be for Palestine or wherever. It'll be for
them. We have to stop them. We have to use their
mentality. The end doesn't always justify the
means, but it damned well does in this case!"

"Do you know where they have found the natural
poison gas?" Mek asked.

"It's radioactive gas. Yes. To within one meter.
GPS."

"Radioactive? They would do that! They would
place radioactive gas in the legislatures of every
country? It is not a natural gas that acts as ricen
does?"

"No. It's radon. It would contaminate an entire

city."

"It would kill the children and women? It isn't something that would only kill the people in the legislature?"

"No. They couldn't hope to deliver anything like that. All they have to do with this is get upwind of any big city and release a hundred pounds of the gas. Everyone close would be killed within a few weeks. The others, it would take years, but they would be doomed."

"Even the Zionist pigs couldn't be that evil! They could not possibly worship a god who would allow such a thing, much less order it!"

"Oh?" Clint asked. "Let's not get into that here. I don't care for the religions of either of you. We have to stop this! We can let the gods, supposing there are any, fight that out among themselves.

"Is there a way you can get to a location in Yemen and do what we call a surgical raid?"

"Yes. Within the hour. I will trust you. You have shown me I cannot trust those who sent me. Tell me where to strike. It will be done. I will also want the websites where you showed me this truth. My friends will need to know those so that they can decide for themselves if this is the will of Allah or of some false god the Zionist pigs have invented!"

Clint wrote the sites on a piece of paper and said

he and Sergio had to view some evidence. They would leave him there in the office for a few minutes. He would understand that he was not to misuse the police computer for any reason.

"I swear by Allah that there will be no *misuse!*"

Clint and Sergio went out to the front, waited ten minutes and went back into the office. Mek was slumped across the desk. There was a note by his hand.

I have taken the dose. I have done what must be done. There will be nothing at that location. I feel you are friends and will intercede with Allah for protection of your souls. There will be another thing soon. You did not ask, but it is the logical thing to end this horror. Adios, amigos – Mek

"Did you expect this?" Sergio asked.

"No. Now we have to wonder what he's set in motion. We also have to do something to make damned sure that gas can't be used in the future!"

"It will always be there. So long as anyone knows it's there the danger is also there. That's what scares me.

"Well, the satellite passes every ninety hours. We have to wait another thirty or so to see what happened to that site."

"And what else may have happened at other sites. I wish I had a clue!"

"I'm afraid I don't care to know where anymore

of your clues will lead.”

“You have to admit. Saving the world from madmen is sort of an exciting way to waste time.”

“Oh, yes. That electrocution thing. Tonio told me about it. I can do with a little less excitement if you would be so kind.”

“Oh, come on! You’d die of boredom if I didn’t do something to break it up now and then!”

“Now and then, okay. All the time, forget it!”

They joked and laughed, but they were also deeply concerned about what may have happened.

They would know in thirty hours. Clint went home. He needed a good long shower, then would go swimming for awhile to relax. He could handle thirty hours of boredom!

He got out of the shower half an hour later and Nito was there with his digital camera. He took a few pictures.

“What’s that for?” Clint asked.

“Those women said they’d give me a dollar apiece for pictures of you like they saw you this morning. I can use the money.”

“They what??! You what?!”

“I don’t get it either, but there are a lot of things you adults do I don’t get. I don’t have much to do here. This will be something.”

“You mean ... you are selling nude pictures of me for a dollar?”

"No. They're pictures of you nude, not nude pictures. I suppose now you'll want a cut! Damn!"

Clint caught on. This was something Tyna put him up to.

"How about if I give some sexy poses. Maybe we can get two dollars a picture."

Nito laughed. "I told her it wouldn't work!"

"Your mother's pretty good, but you took it a little too far."

"Mom? It was Judi. Mom just said it would be fun. She wasn't sure she wanted your picture in everybody's bedroom."

"What did Judi say to that?"

"That they don't need pictures from me. They could come here any morning and take their own. I sort of thought she would think of that."

They joked and went to the deck. Judi was on her deck. Clint took off his bathing suit and said it wasn't necessary to get it wet and posed for a couple of pictures, then Nito stripped and Clint took a couple pictures of him, then they went swimming. Tyna came out onto Judi's deck and they counted, "One. Two. Three!" and gave him the bird. Silvio was passing with a boatload of surfers. He waved and Clint waved back. The surfers started cheering and clapping. Nito went up onto the deck and bowed. He yelled that he had pictures. A dollar apiece, except his dad said to charge two for the sexy ones.

They played awhile in the water. Soon Tyna and Nicole came home and joined them. All-in-all, it was a great afternoon.

The family went into town later. The Rastas from before were gone, but there was another bunch of them near the Mondo Tatu. These were pretty good people and Clint chatted with them for a bit. Ben and Earl, a gay couple from close to Clint's place, came by with Judi. They they all went to Gringos for Mexican food.

They went to the Grill later to chat with friends. Manny, a retired godfather from California (only a very few people knew that) came in and they talked about a number of things. Manny said he had information that a plot by a radical group had been thwarted. He had put something in motion to make things a little safer for a little while. Was that Clint's doing?

"Partly. The one who broke the case is sitting right here."

"Yeah. Judi probably heard a chance remark that gave the whole thing away."

"Nope! Nito heard a chance remark that gave it away!" Clint replied.

"Cripes! Two Judis we don't need! Nobody has any secrets *now*!"

They teased and played until a little after nine,

then went their separate ways.

It wasn't only a great afternoon, it was a great night, too!

Tomorrow night, they would know what had happened at the well site. The way Manny talked it was something that would stop a lot of problems in the future.

Clint spent the following day mostly in his boat with Nito. They went to several islands to visit people and to catch some fish. Nito got a good large lobster near a coral head. They would eat well.

Manny called early to say he had just ordered something that he would tell Clint about. It was something that he knew Clint would want.

Not much exciting happened. The next satellite picture of their spot would be at nine seventeen. The satellite had orders to focus on the designated spot, carefully.

They went into town to El Ultimo Refugio for dinner. Clint would stay when the family went back home to see the satellite view.

They spent a pleasant afternoon. Guillermo, a very handsome Indio man who had figured in the earlier part of this case, came in. Clint asked him if he knew what happened to Randy.

"Yes. He was very nice, but he was too tired and too drunk to be driving."

Clint remembered that Sergio had ordered that nothing be released about the death. He nodded.

Guillermo soon went to talk with two gringas. He would go with both of them. He was a gigolo who made no bones about it. Clint told Tyna about Randy/Ed and the orgy, if he could call it that. She said he was popular with the natives when there were no gringas about.

"All that sex stuff!" Nito said, grinning. "Everybody says Guillermo is the number one stud on the island now that my dad's not in the running anymore. Maybe I can be like him when I get old enough to know what's going on."

"That's nice. Eat your salad," Tyna answered. Clint said he would sleep with guys or chicas, remember that!

"Well, by then I'll be old enough to know if I want that."

They teased about that.

Clint looked around at the people there. His were the only two under about eighteen years of age. Tonight had a lot of gringos in their early twenties. They were playing the same games tourists always were playing, trying to pick up girls. They would be using the standard lines.

Four years old and Nito knew more about sex than they did in an intellectual sense. He didn't have any taboos, but every damned one of them would have.

Life here was good. Life among his people, the

Ngobe, was great!

Nine o'clock curfew siren. Clint would go to the station. Tyna and the kids would go home.

"Can I stay with you, Dad?" Nito asked.

"Okay."

Tyna and Nicole got in a taxi and Clint and Nito went along the street. Half the people they passed knew Clint and greeted them. Nito could join in a conversation like an adult, but usually didn't.

When they got to the police station a couple of blacks were being booked. They were bloody and bruised. They'd been in a fight over who a local black whore was working for. She was sitting there, looking disgusted.

"Hi, Clint! Can you believe those two ugly fat niggers? Think they own me? Who am I working for?

"Shit, man! I work for me and only me! They want to pay me, I work by the hour. I ain't workin' for nobody else! Shit, man!"

"Part of the business," Nito said.

"Ain't that the truth! I got to put up with their shit, like shit! Fuckin' assholes to the last one!"

"They're gay?" Nito asked.

"What? I wouldn't be surprised a second. Why you ask that?"

"You said they're fucking assholes. That usually means gay."

"You, I like. If I wouldn't be past it when you're old enough I'd give you free tickets!"

They joked. Esteban came to ask if she wanted to charge them with anything.

"I ain't done nothing with those two cruds and wouldn't, so I can't charge for it."

"You can go."

"Can I go with her, Dad?"

"She's got business. You'd cramp her style."

"Oh. Right."

She laughed and kissed Nito and went out. She was carrying a radio that was playing the old hippie song, *It's Good News Week.*

Clint and Nito went into Sergio's office and turned on the desk computer. Sergio checked the location figures and put the satellite program on. It went over just three minutes before and the pictures were extremely detailed.

"What the hell! What's that?!" Clint cried.

There were trucks pouring cement into a form that had to be more than a hectare. It was easily six feet thick.

"See if I can focus ... on that sign," Sergio said.

A sign came onto the screen from a slightly side angle. It couldn't quite be read.

"Let me do something," Nito said. He went to the qwerty board to start typing. The sign slowly rotated to where they could make out the words.

They were either in Arabic or Yemeni. Nito fooled around and asked what language it was. Clint said to try Yemeni. He fooled around for a minute and the words came onto the screen in English.

Communications Arabic
Project #243
Relay tower/multinational
Restricted area
Do Not Enter
"Bringing the world together"

"I'll be damned! That must be what Manny said he was doing. The entire part of that hill will be covered in thick reinforced concrete and a tower and automatic relay station will be on it. Nothing will leak and no one will know that's a radioactive site under it for a hundred years or more!"

"Well, that's one that came out right enough! No one's going to drill for radon gas there!" Sergio agreed. "We'll just have to wait to see what else Mek put in motion. I suppose when we hear about it we'll know it was him."

Clint and Nito went home. Clint told Tyna what had happened and she sighed in relief. "When something had you scared like that it had me terrified!"

"You knew I was scared? You were terrified?"

"Come on! When you were so casual it could put

Page 57

me to sleep, then forgot and came out here with those women sitting around? Nude? What? I'm stupid?"

"I guess it was a lot more obvious than I wanted it to be."

They talked about it for a little while longer, then started their play and teasing. Nito said it was sex time and took Nicole to their bedroom.

It was a truly wonderful night.

The next two days went very smoothly. They didn't hear anything about Yemen and no news on the computers. Clint was wondering if Mek had done something they wouldn't ever hear about. It was certain to be something that would have some very powerful and very long-lasting results. He couldn't find anything more about Mek or who he was, though he spent a lot of time trying.

The next day the family were in Gringos for lunch. The news was on the TV about some kind of accident where a large cruise boat had run into a smaller cabin cruiser and four young people were killed. They weren't paying much attention.

Clint glanced up just as the news from other places was moving in script across the bottom of the screen: ... *was a serious blow to the hospital community in Israel. The seven doctors who had formed the group are thought to all be dead from the blast at this time ... Waterford, England. A man on a rampage has shot and killed six people in a supermarket ...*

Clint didn't say anything. He would investigate that story when he got home. It would be on the TVN website.

They had a good lunch and went into town for Tyna to shop while Clint and the kids played in the park. A number of people stopped to chat and two gringas tried to pick Clint up. Nito said they would have to wait until his wife, his mother, wasn't going to come along at any minute to get laid by his dad.

"Is he serious?!" one of them cried.

"Serious? I guess so. Tyna's shopping in the China. Why?"

They didn't quite know how to take that. They left, not knowing whether to laugh or what.

Nito laughed when they were gone. "Did you see the look on the blond's face? She looked like I had pinched her in the ass!"

"You're too much sometimes."

"I try!"

They laughed and played. The girls came back through and stopped. "I guess we really made silly stupid fools out of ourselves. I apologize," the blond said.

"Oh, don't worry. Fifty women a day try to get

my dad to lay them. He doesn't, but you should meet Guillermo. He's famous."

"Guillermo?"

"Indio. Knock down dead handsome and gigolo who makes it plain from the first that's what he's doing. Everyone says he's the greatest lover on the island," Clint answered.

"That god outside the airport? We saw him right away. He was with another bitch who got off the plane just before us. She's got money up the ass and gets what she wants. We're low budget."

"Guillermo's not too expensive," Nito said. "It's first come, first serviced."

"It's first come, first ... you're thirty years old and disguised as a kid, right?" the brunette asked.

They laughed. Tyna came up and asked what was going on. Nito said the girls wanted Dad to lay them, but he wouldn't.

"This is your wife? I don't blame you!" the blond cried. "I'd kill for hair like that! Are you an Indian?"

"India? Yes. Clint's Ngobe, same as me."

"Oh, my god! Clint? Clint Faraday? I'm a friend of Gina Merkel! She stayed with you for two nights about six years ago! She said you were the best.... Oh, sorry. I should keep my mouth shut!"

"Everybody knows Clint was no virgin when we met," Tyna said, with a laugh. "He had quite the reputation as a ladies man.

"Hon, we'd better get back. Ben and Earl are coming over for supper. I want to cook something special. I'm in a competition with Earl for who can make the best dish."

"Ben and Earl? And we're two gringas on the make? Hint! Hint!" the brunette said.

"They're gay, so I guess you'll have to stay horny," Nito said. They all laughed. "Our luck sucks," the blond said.

"So do they," Nito fired back, which really got a laugh.

Clint and family went back to the house. Clint went to the computer to bring up TVNnews.com. He found the story:

Haifa, Israel: A medical research group, The Medicalistic Research Group, Ltd., was meeting in their headquarters in this city today when a suicide bomber burst into the conference room where they were holding their quarterly directors' meeting and set off a bomb that broke windows two blocks away. The incident was a serious blow to....

So. That was what Mek had set up. Hopefully, there would be no further action using radon gas. It wasn't likely there was another well that could produce the gas in nearly the quantity that one could. The world had enough problems without that kind of threat available.

Clint thought about a weapon Dave had given – loaned – to some Indios a few years ago. It could be devastating, if in a more directable way. It was another thing that could be brought out at any time. This one couldn't. The need of that kind of source of anything that deadly meant it would be rare or never for it to happen again.

The end justifies the means in a very few cases. This was one of them.

What kind of sick world would his progeny have to face?

It was a very scary thing to contemplate.

Good news week. All-in-all, it was that!

C. D. Moulton's works are available on most major outlets as printed or e-books. CD writes the CD Grimes, PI, mysteries, the Det. Lt. Nick Storie mysteries, the Clint Faraday mysteries, the Flight of the Maita science fiction series, books on orchid culture and many others of many types. Mystery, adventure, intrigue, science fiction, humor, fantasy, paranormal, mild erotica, and factual.